SHOESHINE WHITTAKER

HELEN KETTEMAN

Illustrations by
SCOTT GOTO

Walker & Company

New York

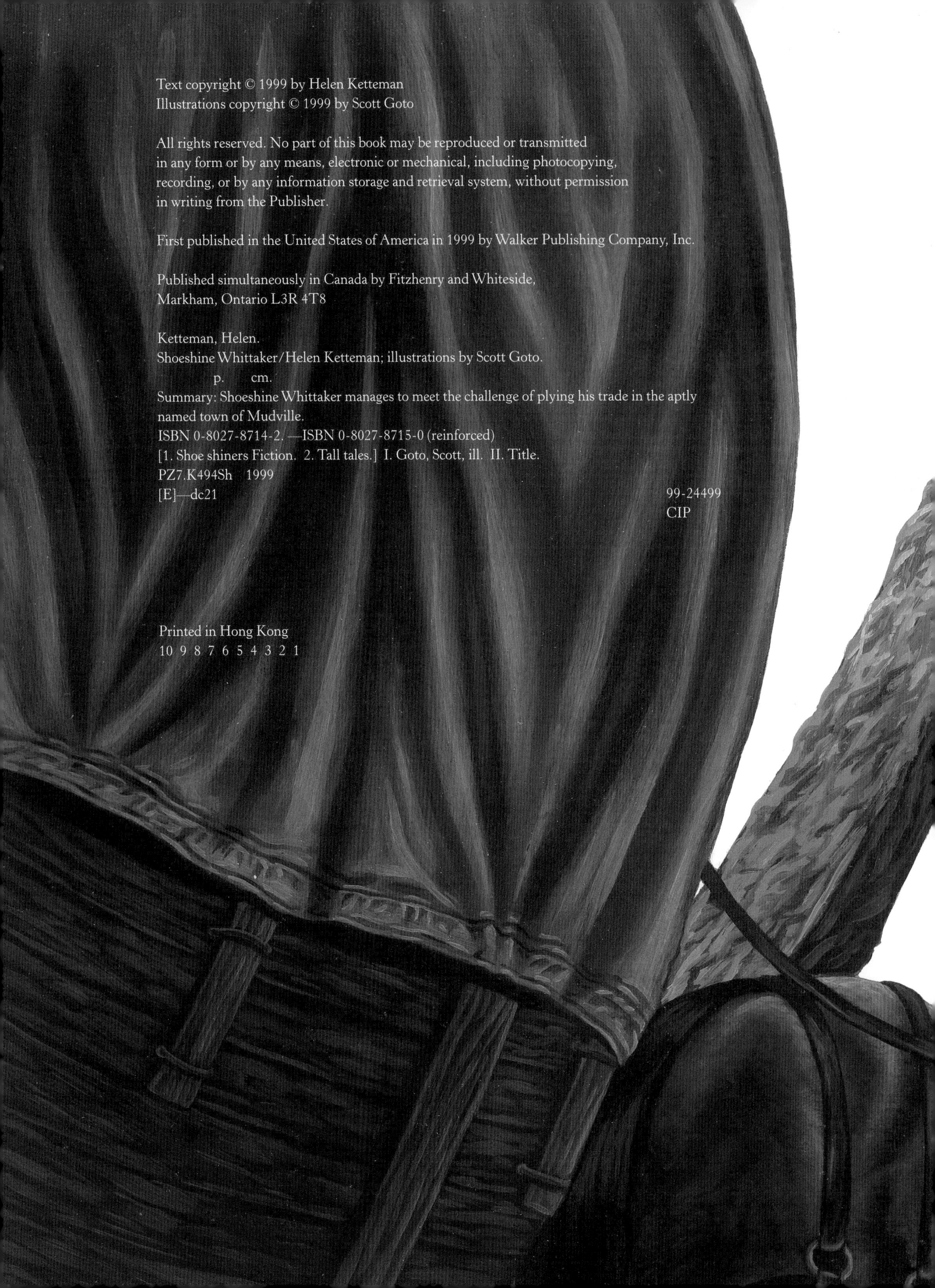

First published in the United States of America in 1999 by Walker Publishing Company, Inc.

Published simultaneously in Canada by Fitzhenry and Whiteside,
Markham, Ontario L3R 4T8

Ketteman, Helen.
Shoeshine Whittaker/Helen Ketteman; illustrations by Scott Goto.
p. cm.
Summary: Shoeshine Whittaker manages to meet the challenge of plying his trade in the aptly named town of Mudville.
ISBN 0-8027-8714-2. —ISBN 0-8027-8715-0 (reinforced)
[1. Shoe shiners Fiction. 2. Tall tales.] I. Goto, Scott, ill. II. Title.
PZ7.K494Sh 1999
[E]—dc21 99-24499
CIP

Printed in Hong Kong
10 9 8 7 6 5 4 3 2 1

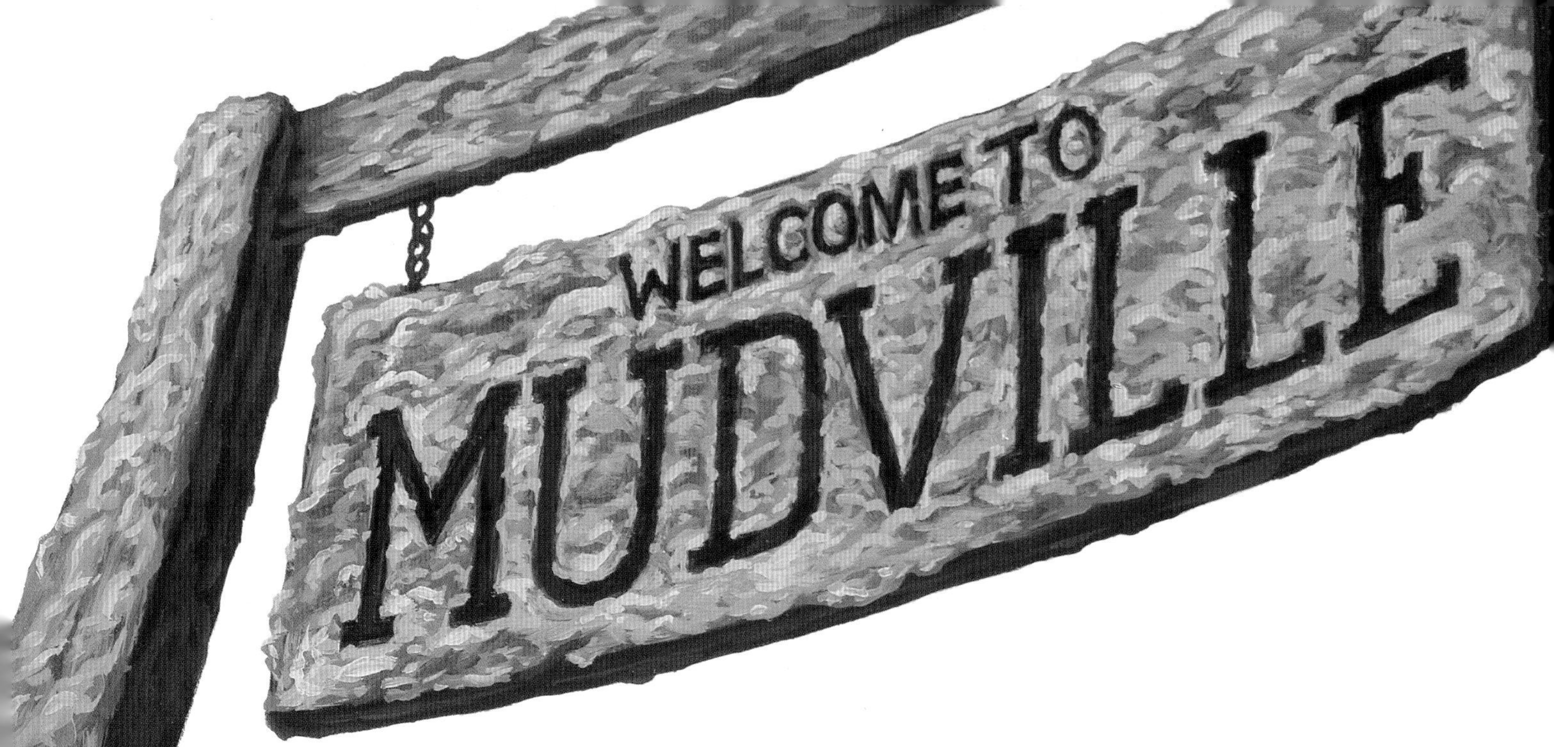
WELCOME TO
MUDVILLE

To all the great librarians
in Texas
—H. K.

For my family
and friends
—S. G.

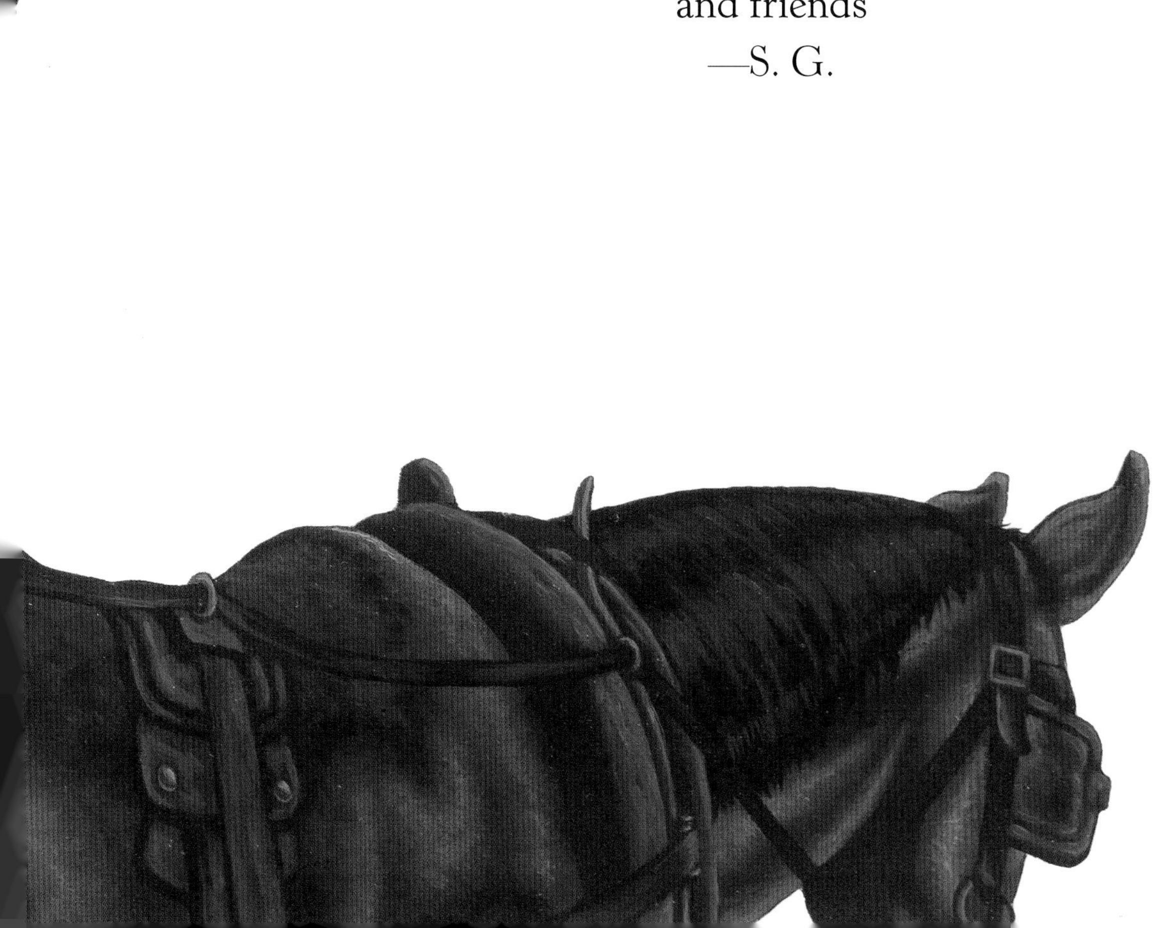

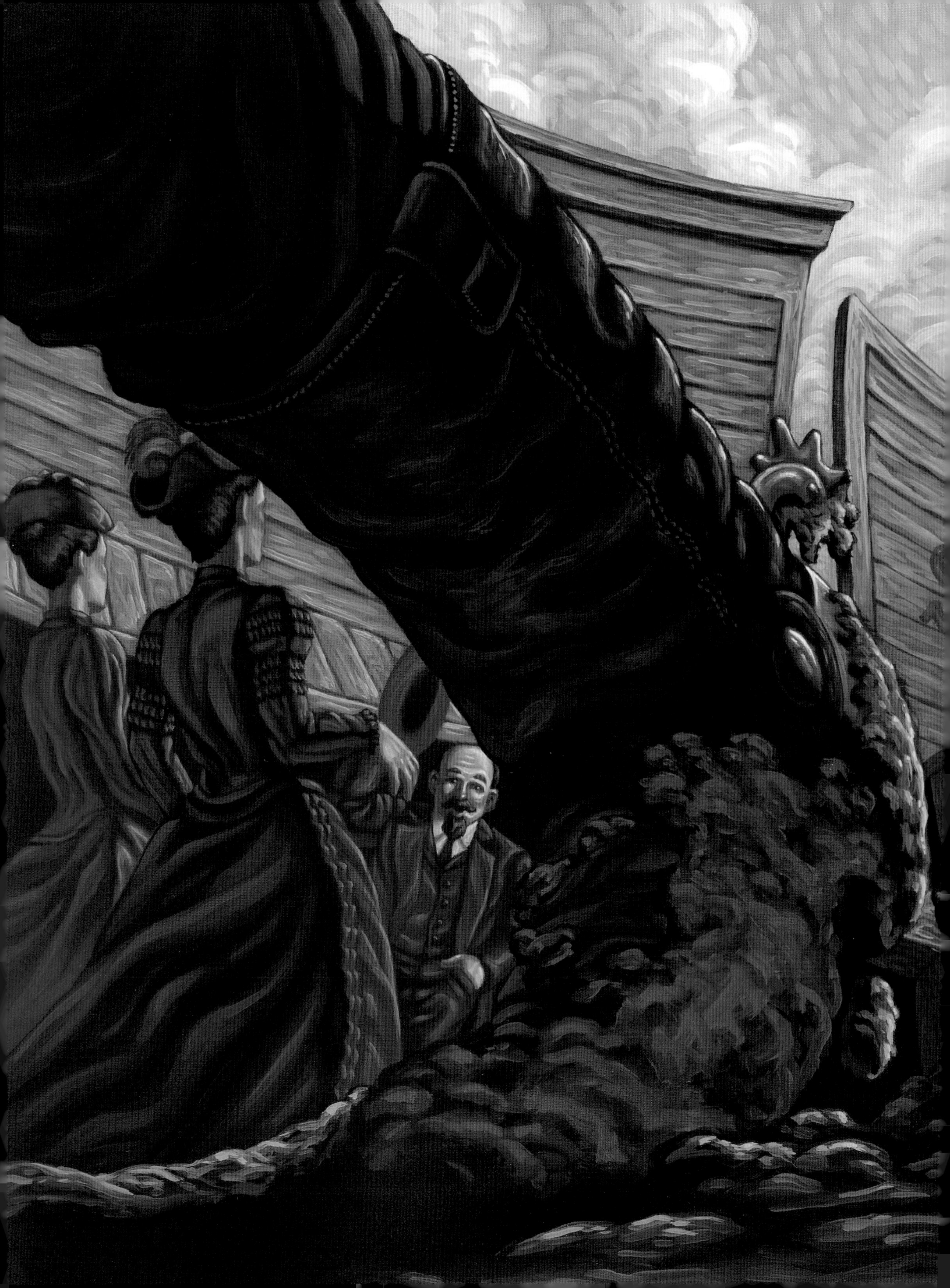

Mudville sat on the banks of Mud River, which overflowed ever' single time it rained. That was one dirty town, all right. The streets were muddy, the wooden sidewalks were cruddy, the houses were dusty, and the people's shoes were crusty. Reckon any other town would have been downright disgraced with such a look, but, shoot, this was Mudville, after all.

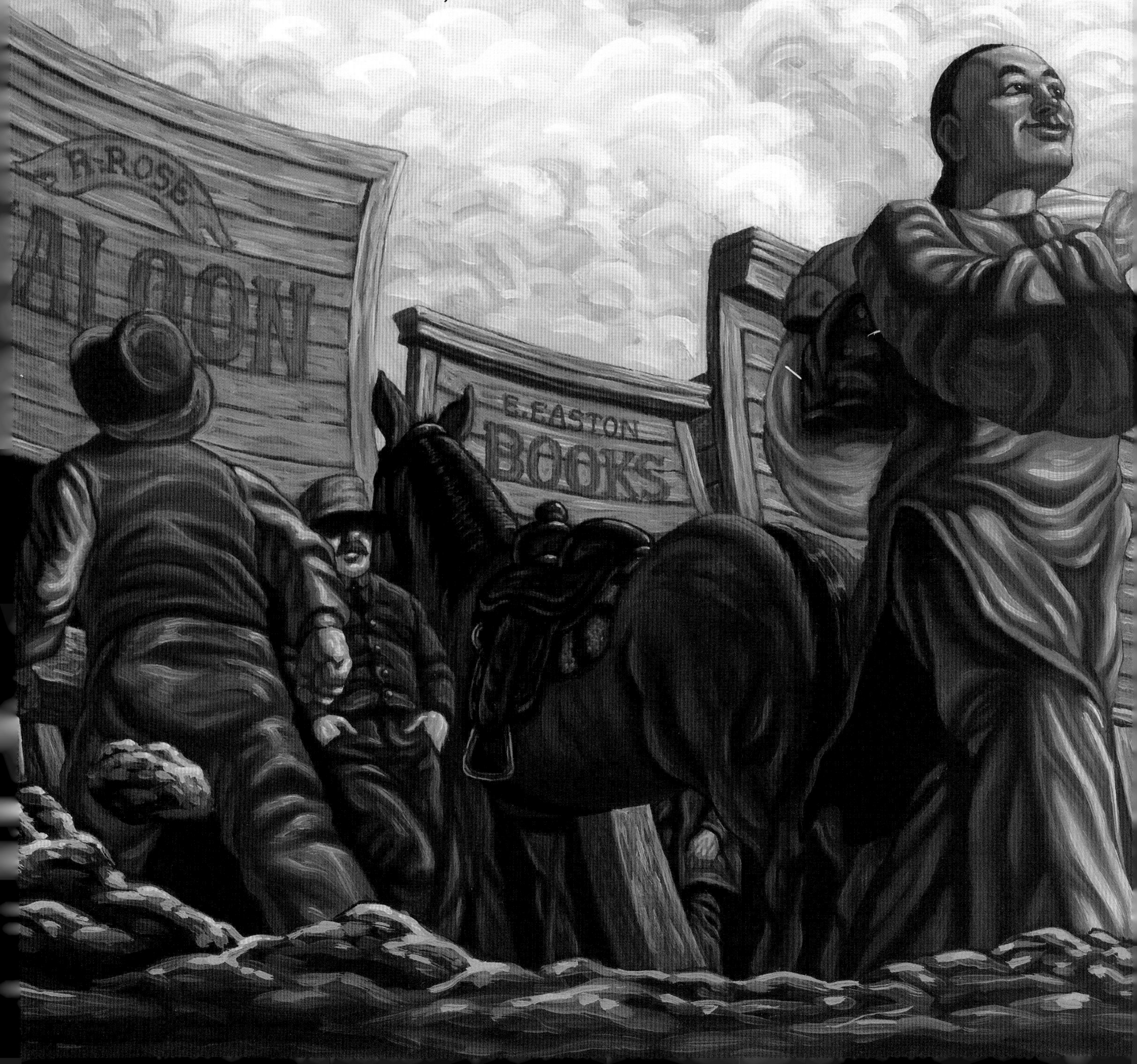
H.ROSE
E.EASTON
BOOKS

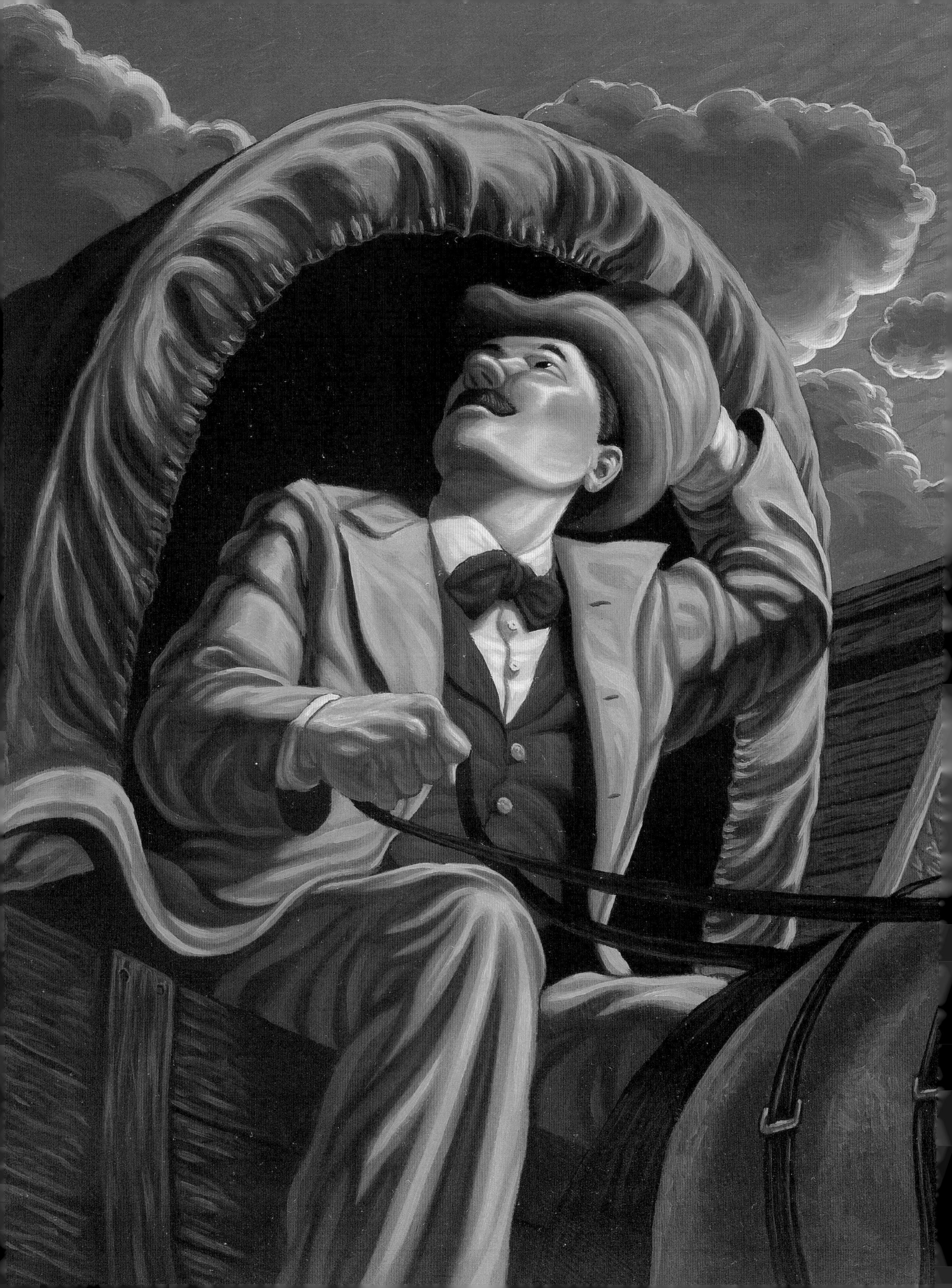

'Long about daybreak one morning, Shoeshine Whittaker drove his wagon into town. It bumped along Main Street, throwing clumps of dried mud in the air. Seein' ever'thing so dirty pleased Shoeshine no end, and he pulled his horse to a stop at Fanny Ambrose's Fine Eating Establishment.

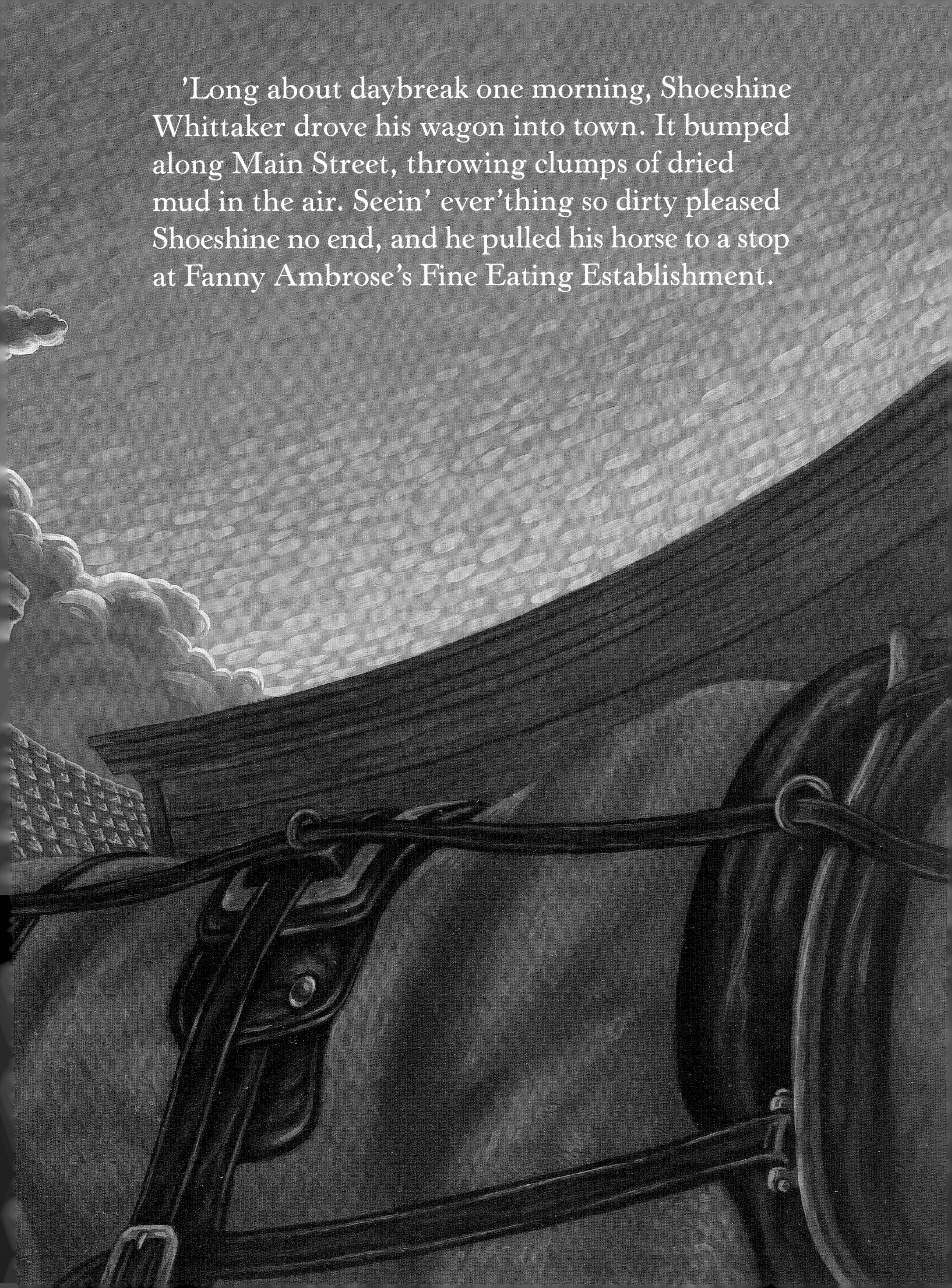

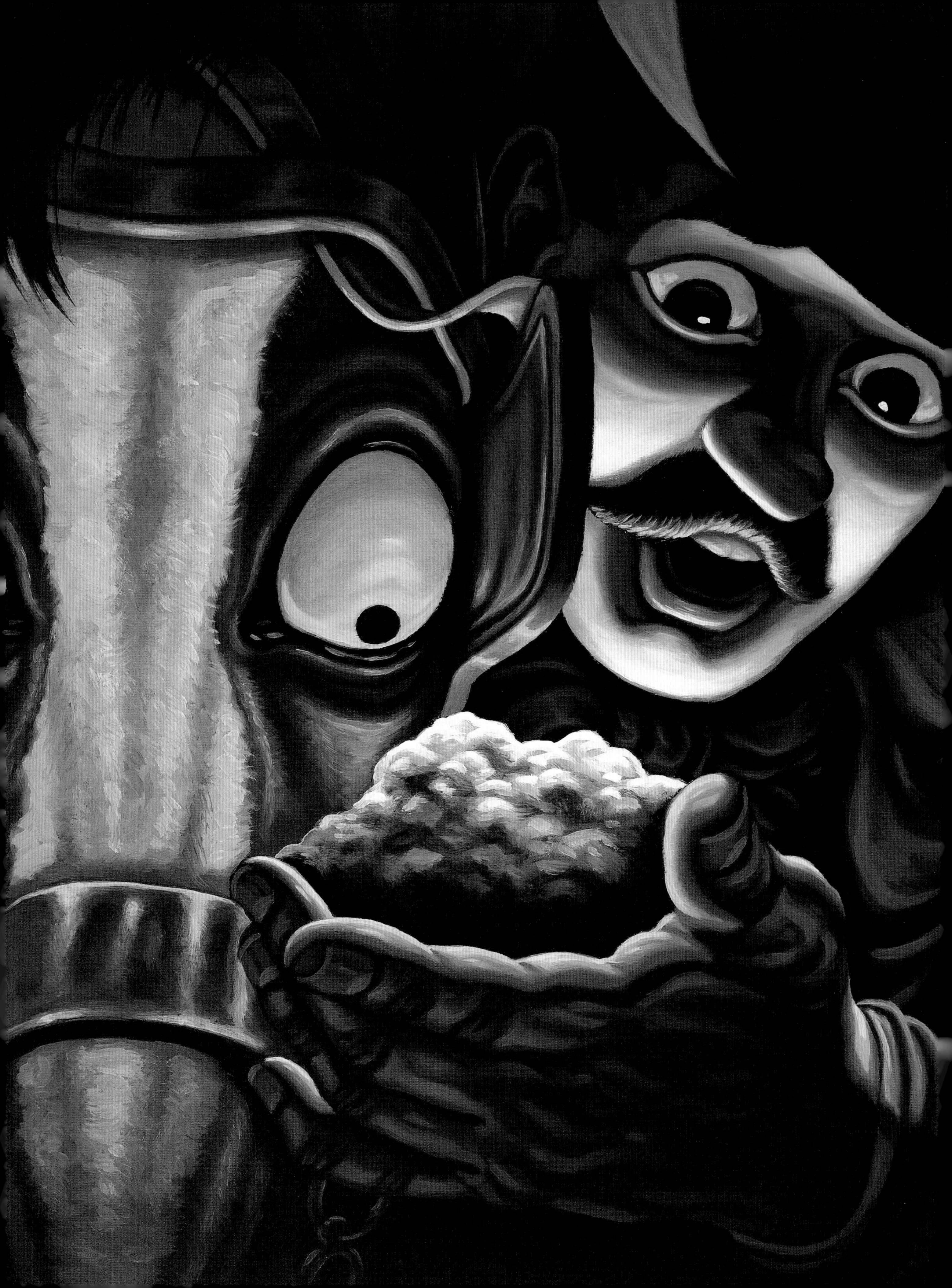

Shoeshine jumped off his wagon, picked up
a dirt clod, and held it up to his horse. "This may
look like plain dirt, Miss Clara, but I reckon it's
pay dirt to us." Shoeshine unloaded his wagon
and began settin' up for business.

Wasn't long 'fore people started stirrin', and
pretty soon, Sheriff Blackstone mosied up. "Who
might you be, stranger, and what's this stuff you got
spread all over our sidewalk?"

Shoeshine waved his top hat with a flourish, and bowed. "Shoeshine's the name, and shoeshine's the game. I figure I've come just in the nick of time."

Sheriff Blackstone narrowed his eyes. "What in thunderation are you talkin' about? Nick of time for what?"

Shoeshine pointed to the sheriff's boots. "In the nick of time to save those from the dry rot. You got to take care of your boots, Sheriff, or they're like to fall apart on you. Have a seat and I'll show you what I mean."

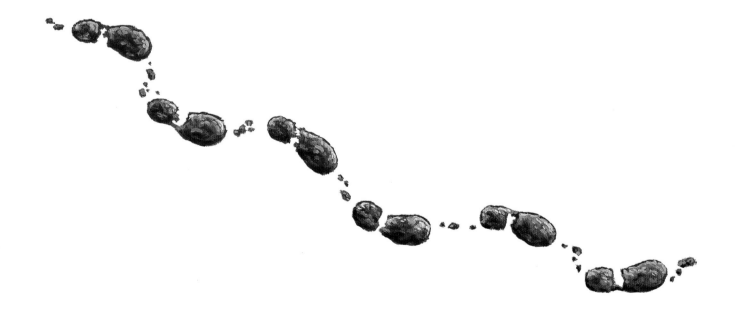

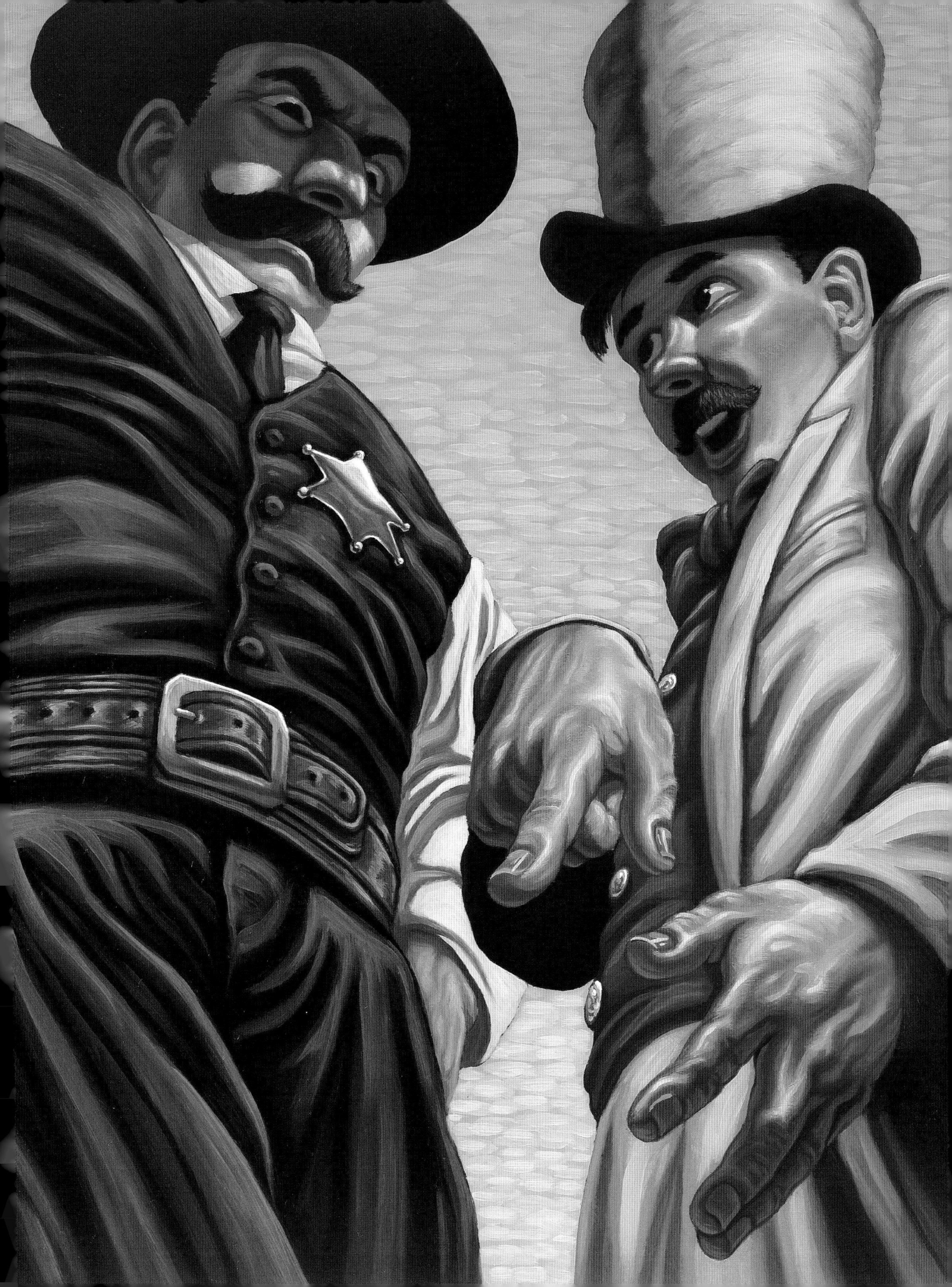

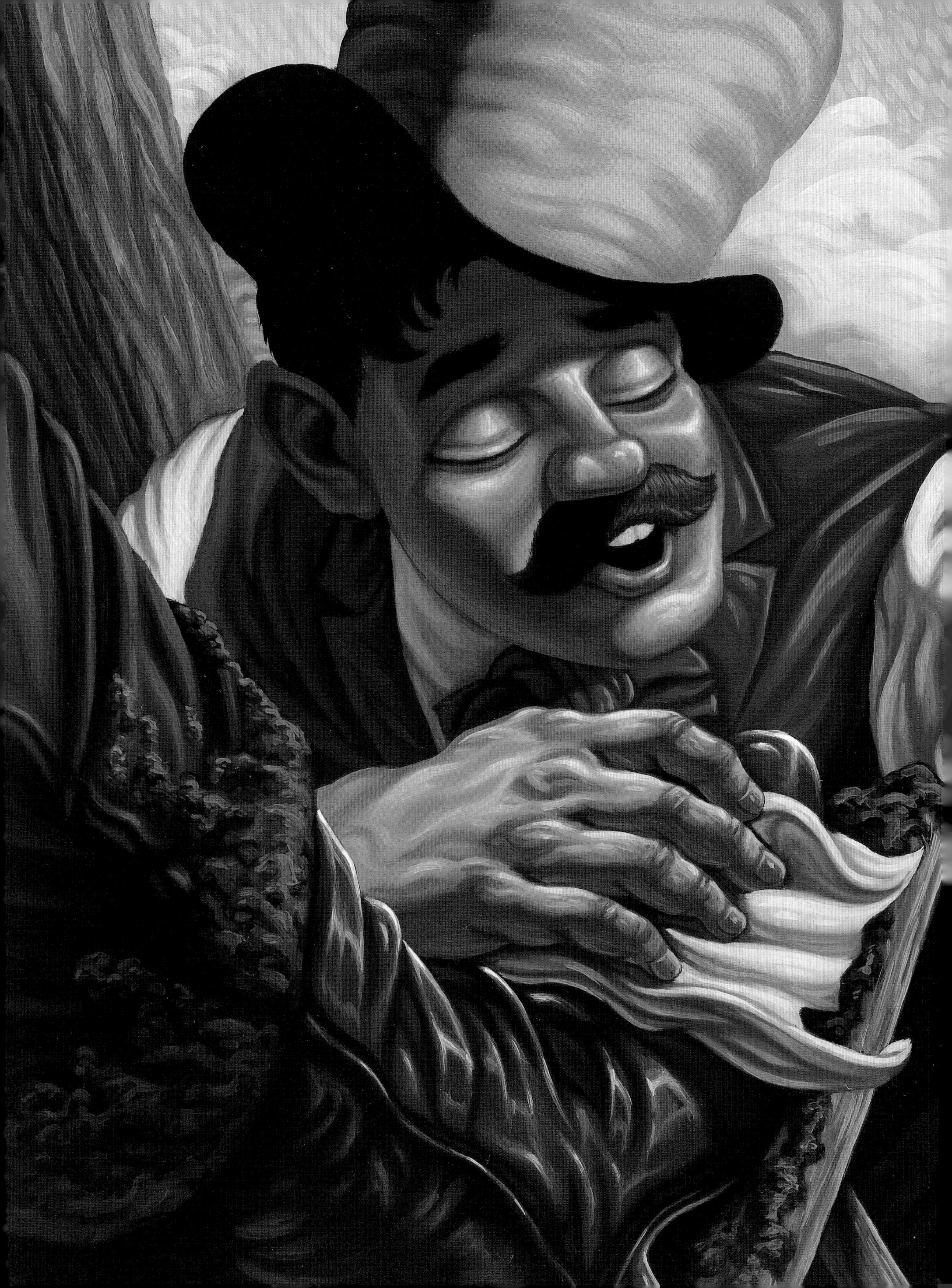

A crowd gathered as Shoeshine rolled up his
sleeves and brushed clumps of mud off the sheriff's
boots. Then he opened a tin of polish and rubbed
and scrubbed. Finally, he slapped his rags across the
boots and stood back. "That, Sheriff, is a shoeshine.
Looks purty, and it'll protect your boots, too."

The crowd gasped. Sheriff Blackstone blinked.
"Why, my boots are shiny as a mail-order mirror!"

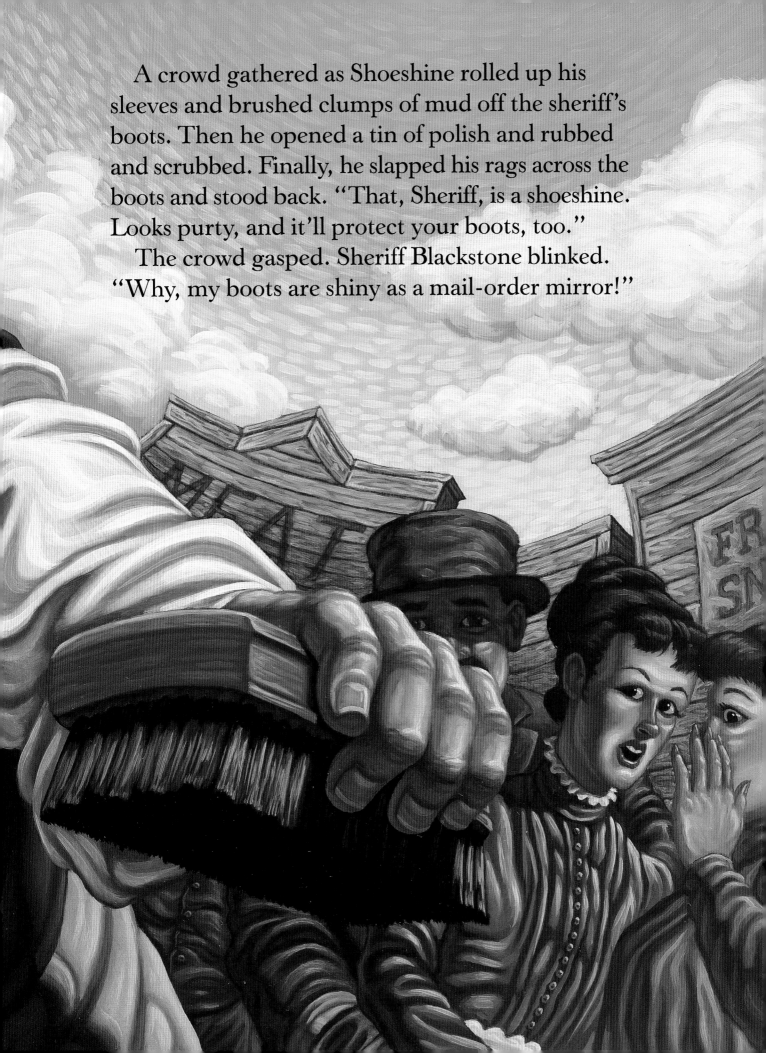

"Don't be shy folks, step right up!" Shoeshine said, pointing to his sign. "Shoeshine Whittaker will give you the finest shoeshine in the West!"

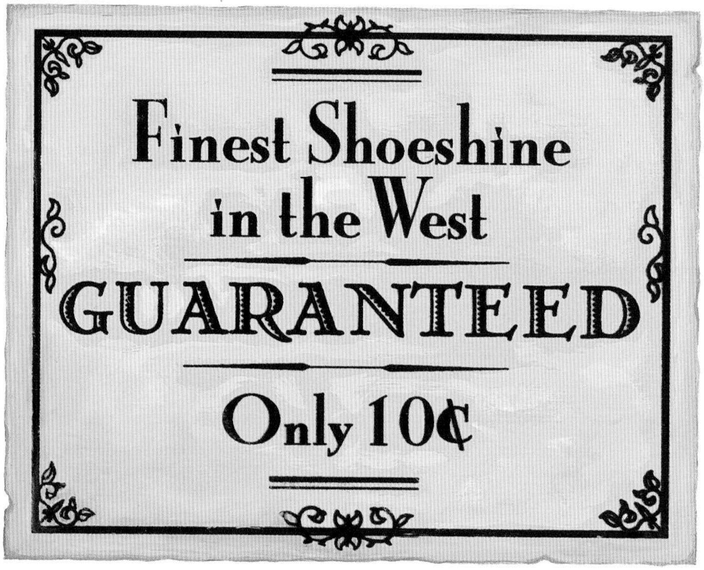
Finest Shoeshine
in the West
GUARANTEED
Only 10¢

Soon the whole town was lined up for shoeshines. By the end of the day, ever' person in Mudville had beautiful, shiny boots.

Shoeshine Whittaker counted his money. "Forty dollars and fifty cents! Miss Clara, we've struck it rich." Shoeshine rode out of town to set up camp for the night before movin' on.

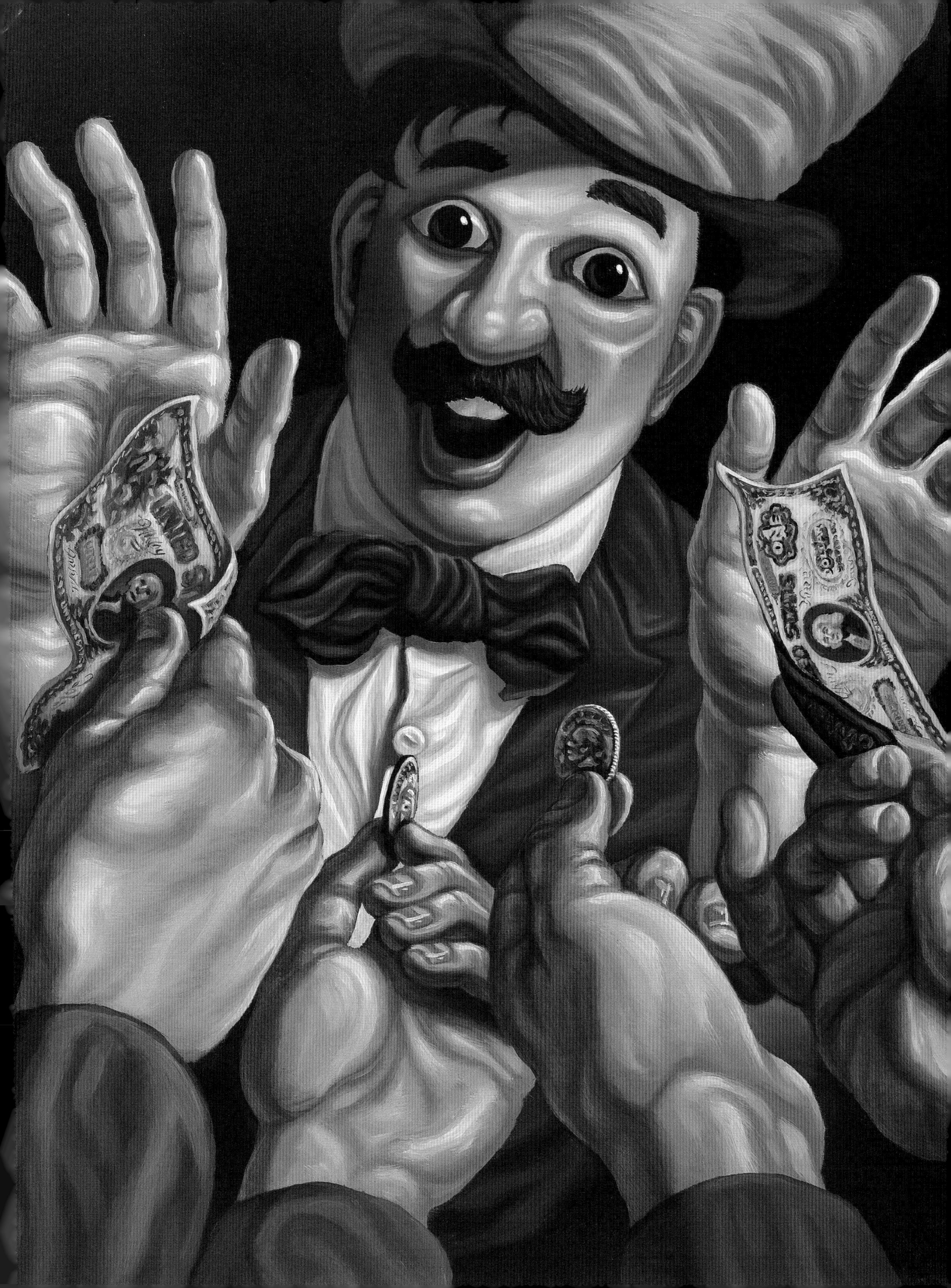

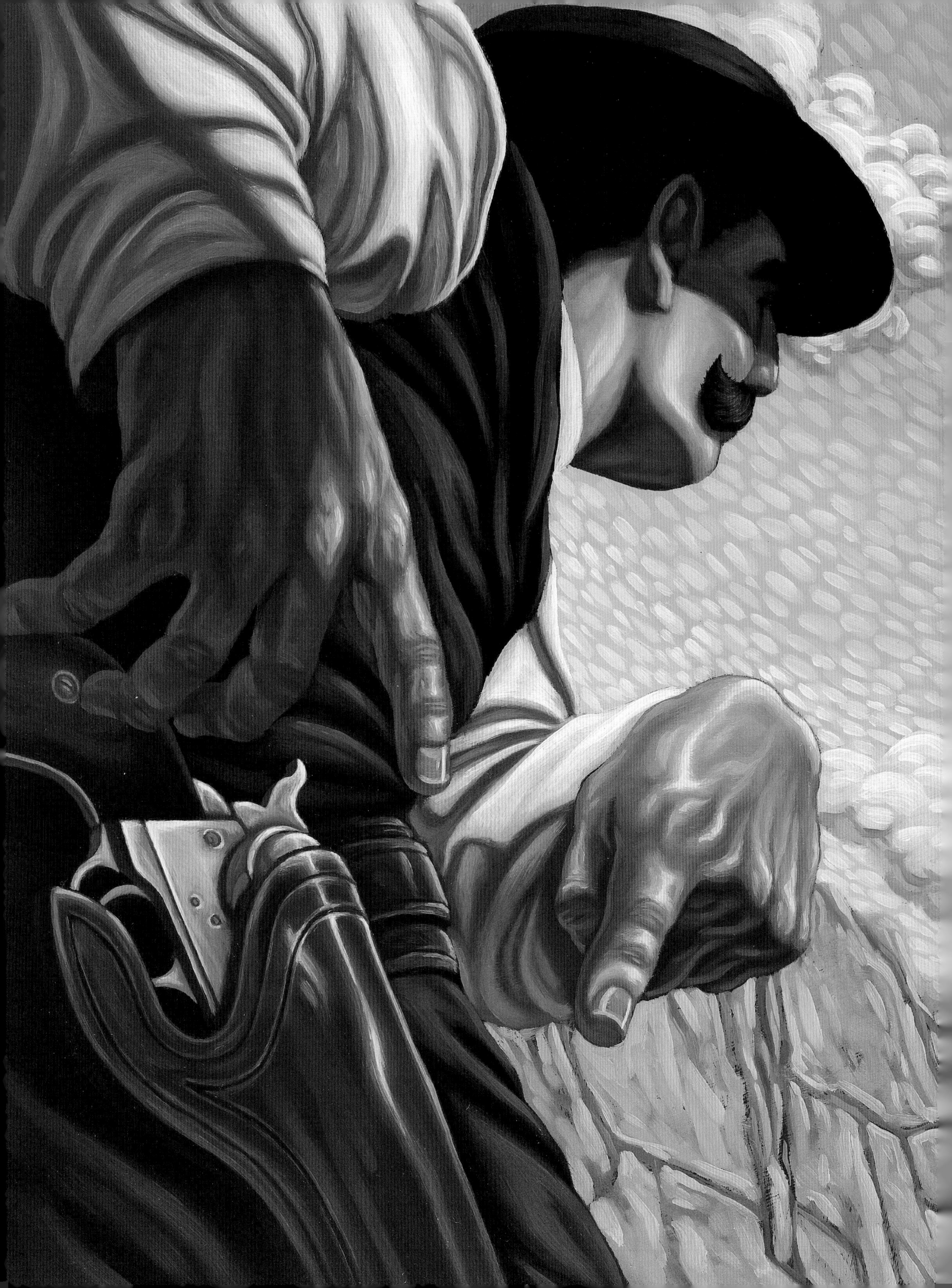

But early the next mornin', the sheriff shook Shoeshine awake.

"What's wrong, Sheriff?" asked Shoeshine, climbing out of his wagon.

"You're lower than a snake's belly, you underhanded vermin, that's what's wrong," said the sheriff. "There ain't a shiny boot left in town, and your sign said guaranteed. You're under arrest for cheatin' the fine folks of Mudville."

"Sheriff, I can't guarantee people's shoes will *stay* shiny!" Shoeshine said.

"Your sign said guaranteed. 'Less those shoes stay shiny, you'll have to face Judge Hangin' Harry in court."

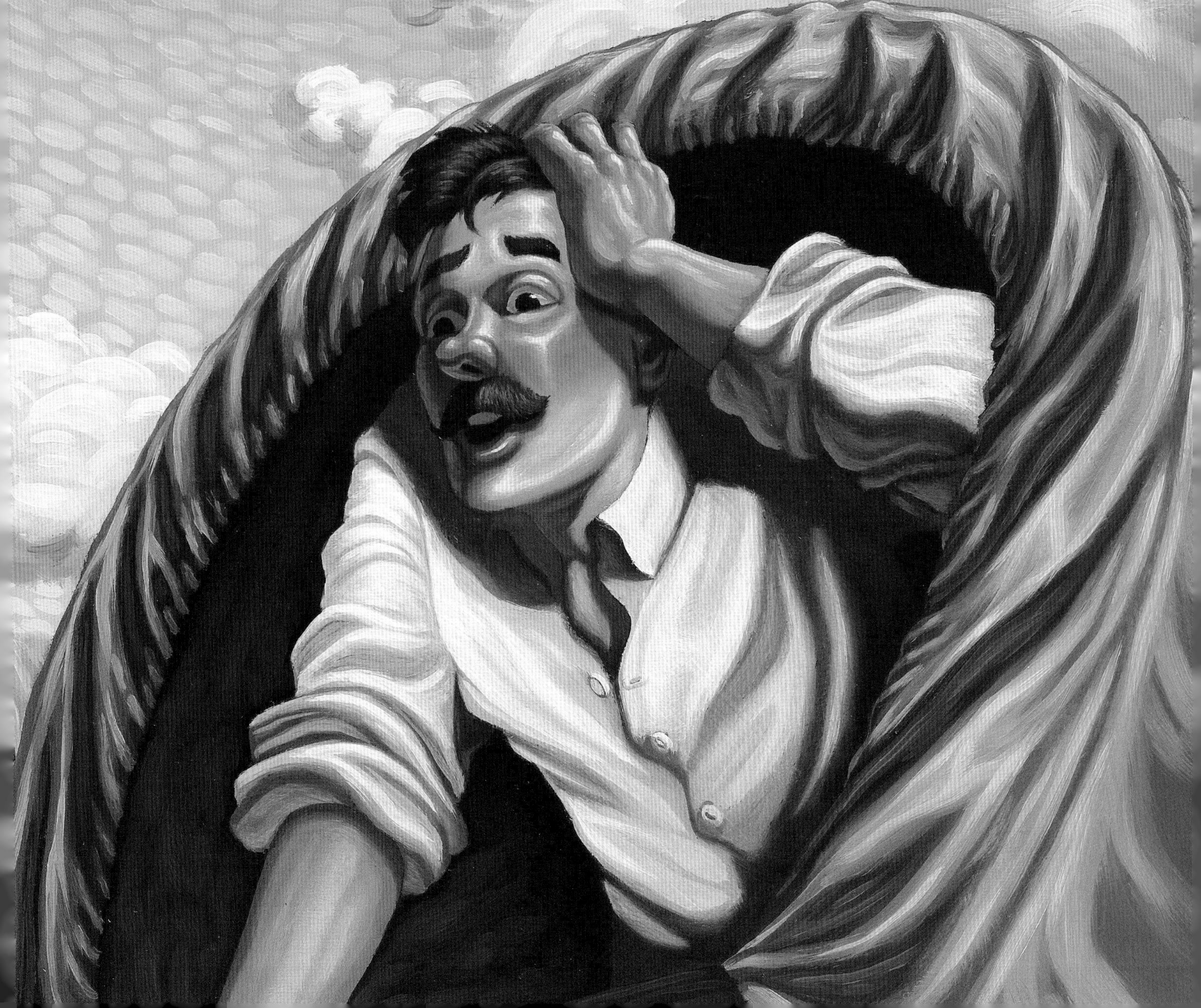

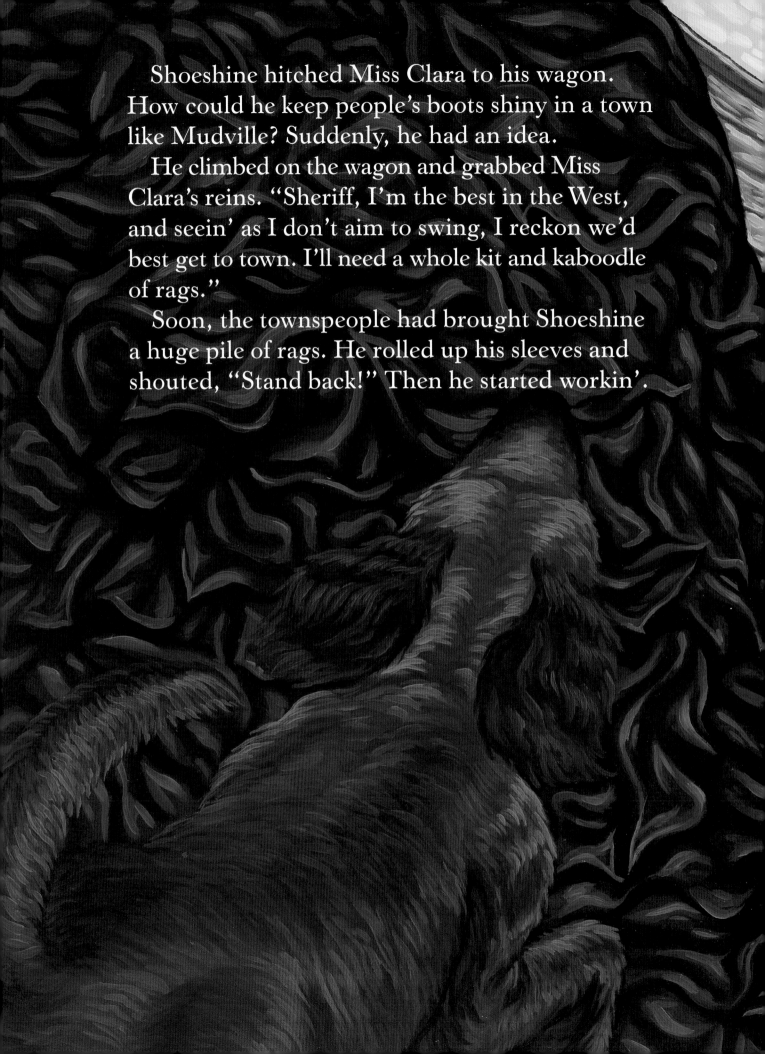

Shoeshine hitched Miss Clara to his wagon.
How could he keep people's boots shiny in a town
like Mudville? Suddenly, he had an idea.

He climbed on the wagon and grabbed Miss
Clara's reins. "Sheriff, I'm the best in the West,
and seein' as I don't aim to swing, I reckon we'd
best get to town. I'll need a whole kit and kaboodle
of rags."

Soon, the townspeople had brought Shoeshine
a huge pile of rags. He rolled up his sleeves and
shouted, "Stand back!" Then he started workin'.

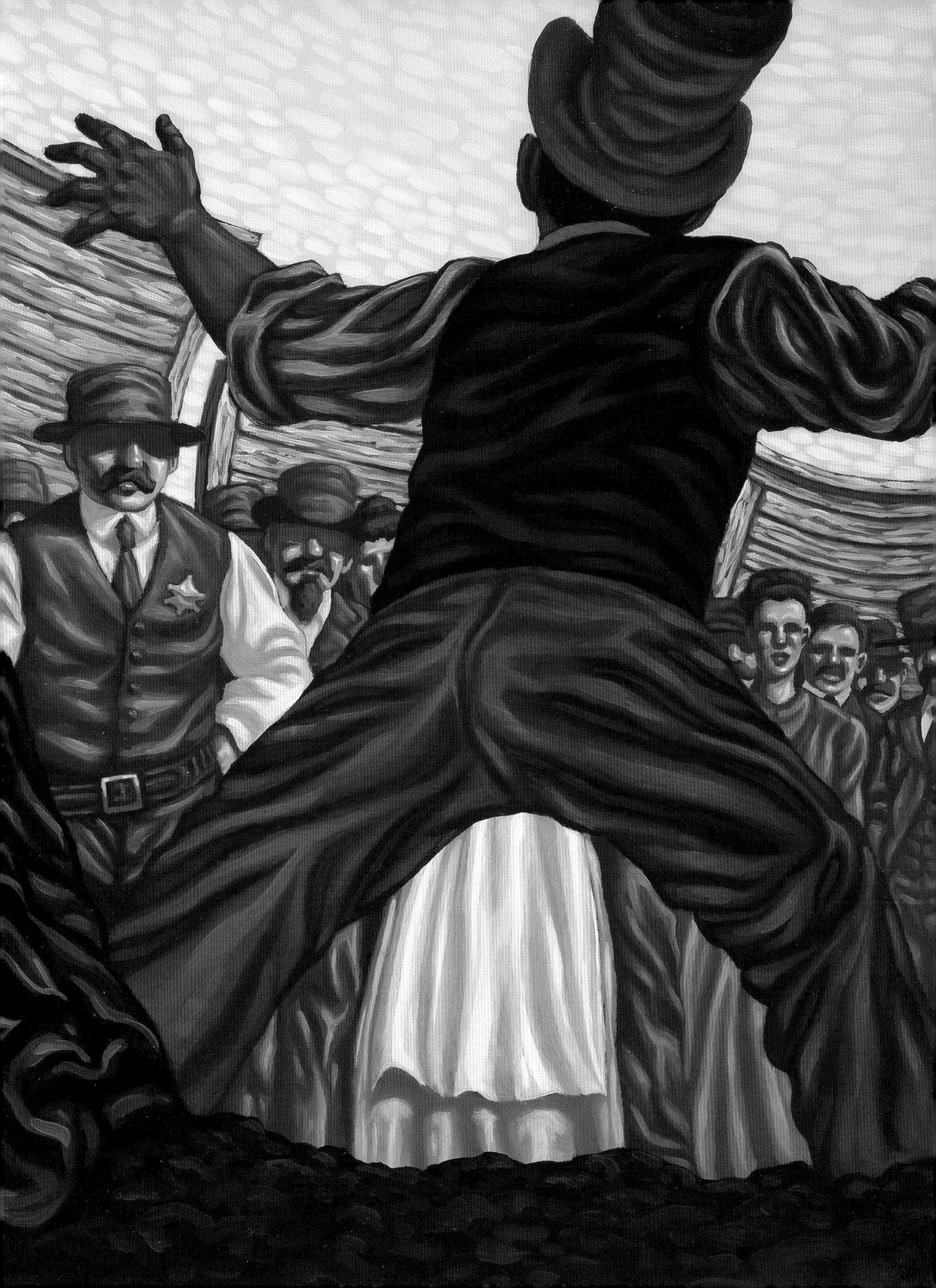

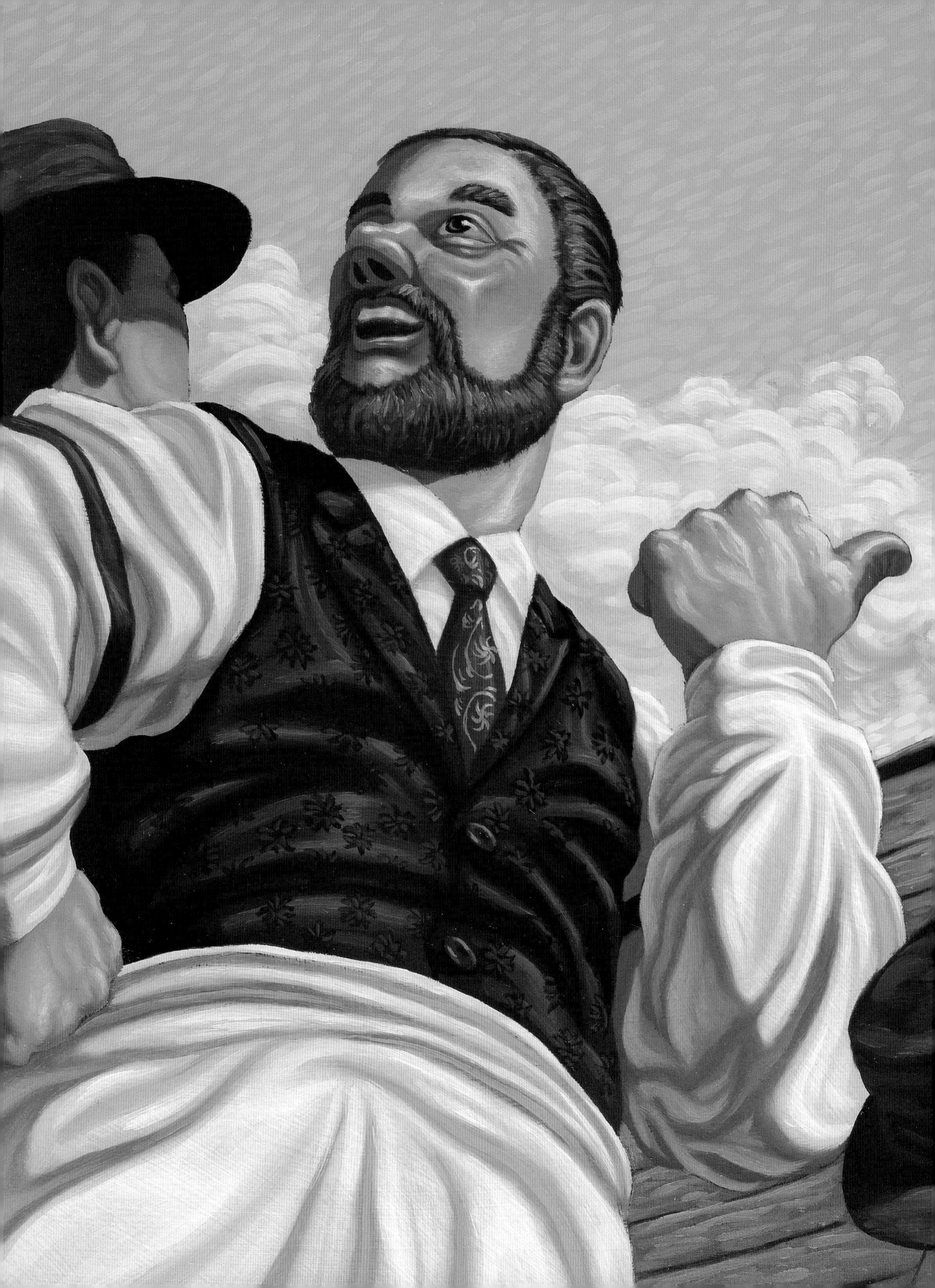

He rubbed and scrubbed and shined and polished. By noon, Mudville City Jail and Stable sparkled in the sun, and Hayden Clopstop's General Dry Goods and Dentist's Office shone a bright cornflower blue. Even Hayden Clopstop himself was surprised.

"I plumb disremembered it was blue," he said.

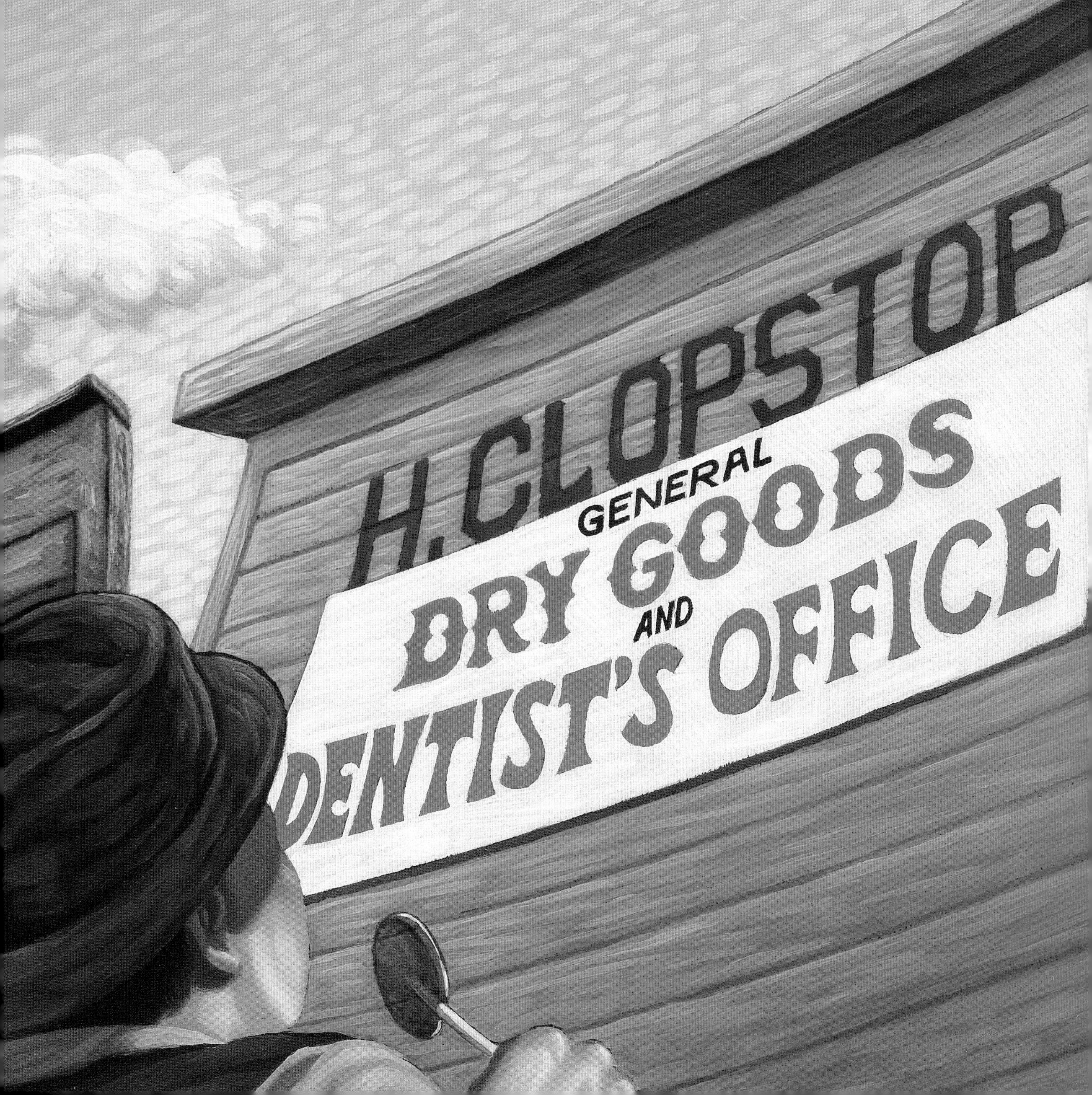
H. CLOPSTOP
GENERAL
DRY GOODS
AND
DENTIST'S OFFICE

All afternoon, Shoeshine polished and rubbed. By sunset, half the houses and sidewalks gleamed shinier than a new twenty-dollar gold piece.

The sun set, but Shoeshine kept workin'. He scrubbed by moonlight all night long.

By mornin', even the dirt road of Main Street was glistenin'. Why, there wasn't a speck of dust or a spot of loose dirt to be seen.

The townspeople couldn't believe their eyes. Mudville had never looked like this!

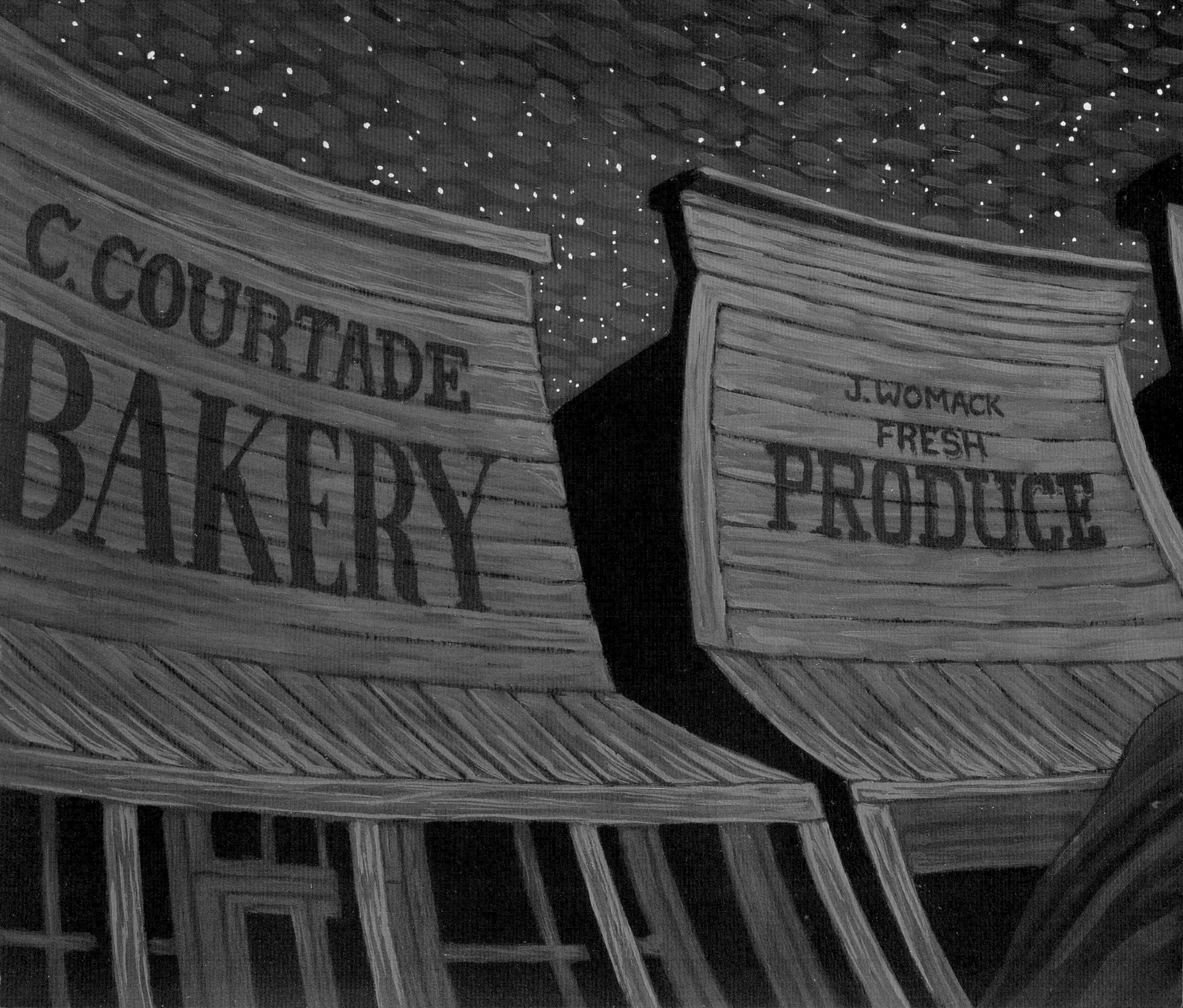
C. COURTADE
BAKERY
J. WOMACK
FRESH
PRODUCE

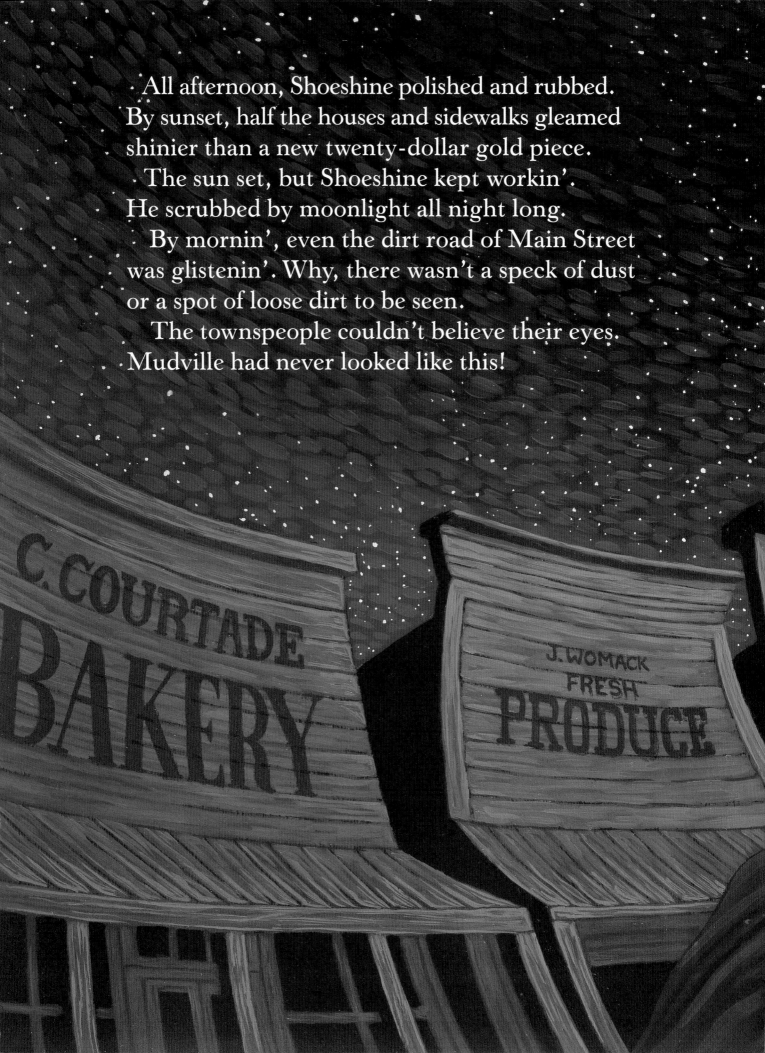

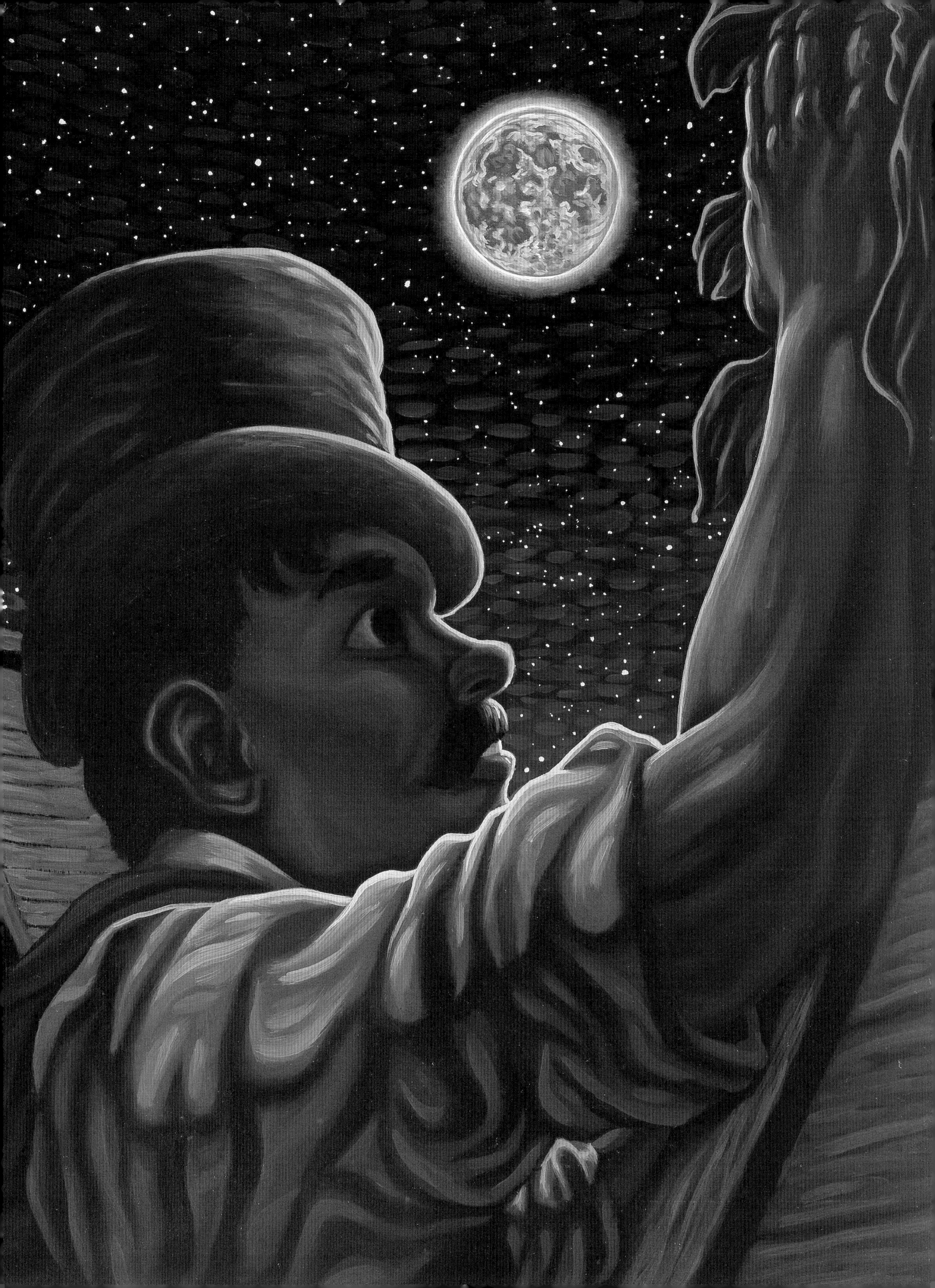

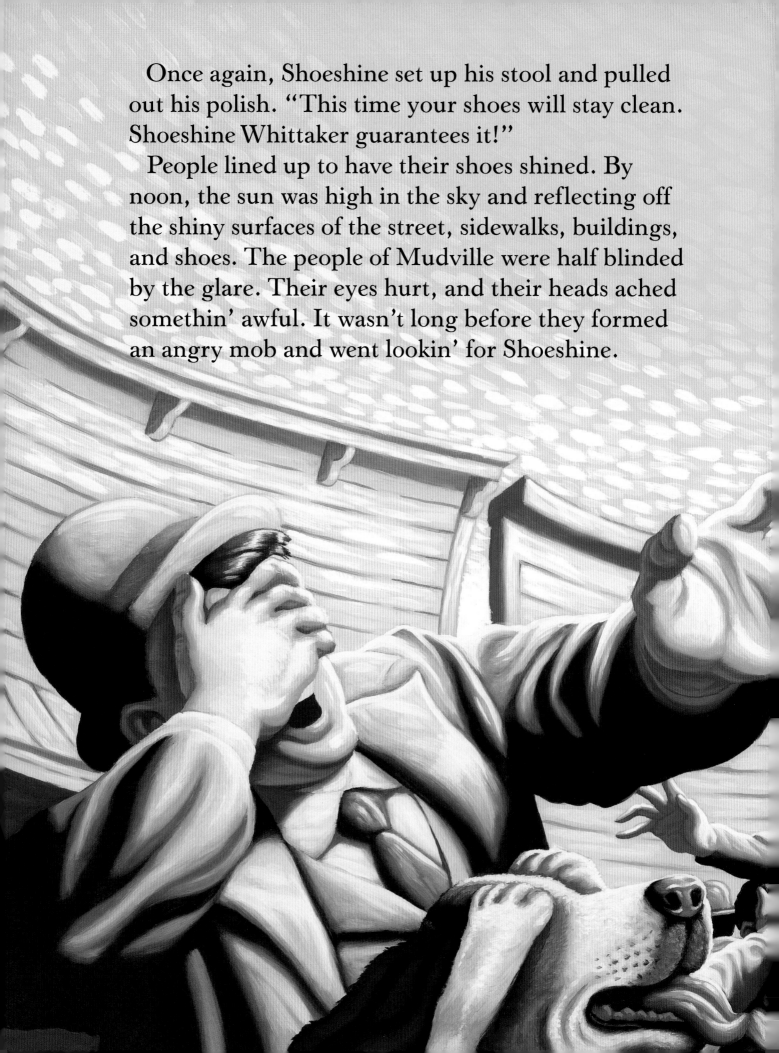

Once again, Shoeshine set up his stool and pulled out his polish. "This time your shoes will stay clean. Shoeshine Whittaker guarantees it!"

People lined up to have their shoes shined. By noon, the sun was high in the sky and reflecting off the shiny surfaces of the street, sidewalks, buildings, and shoes. The people of Mudville were half blinded by the glare. Their eyes hurt, and their heads ached somethin' awful. It wasn't long before they formed an angry mob and went lookin' for Shoeshine.

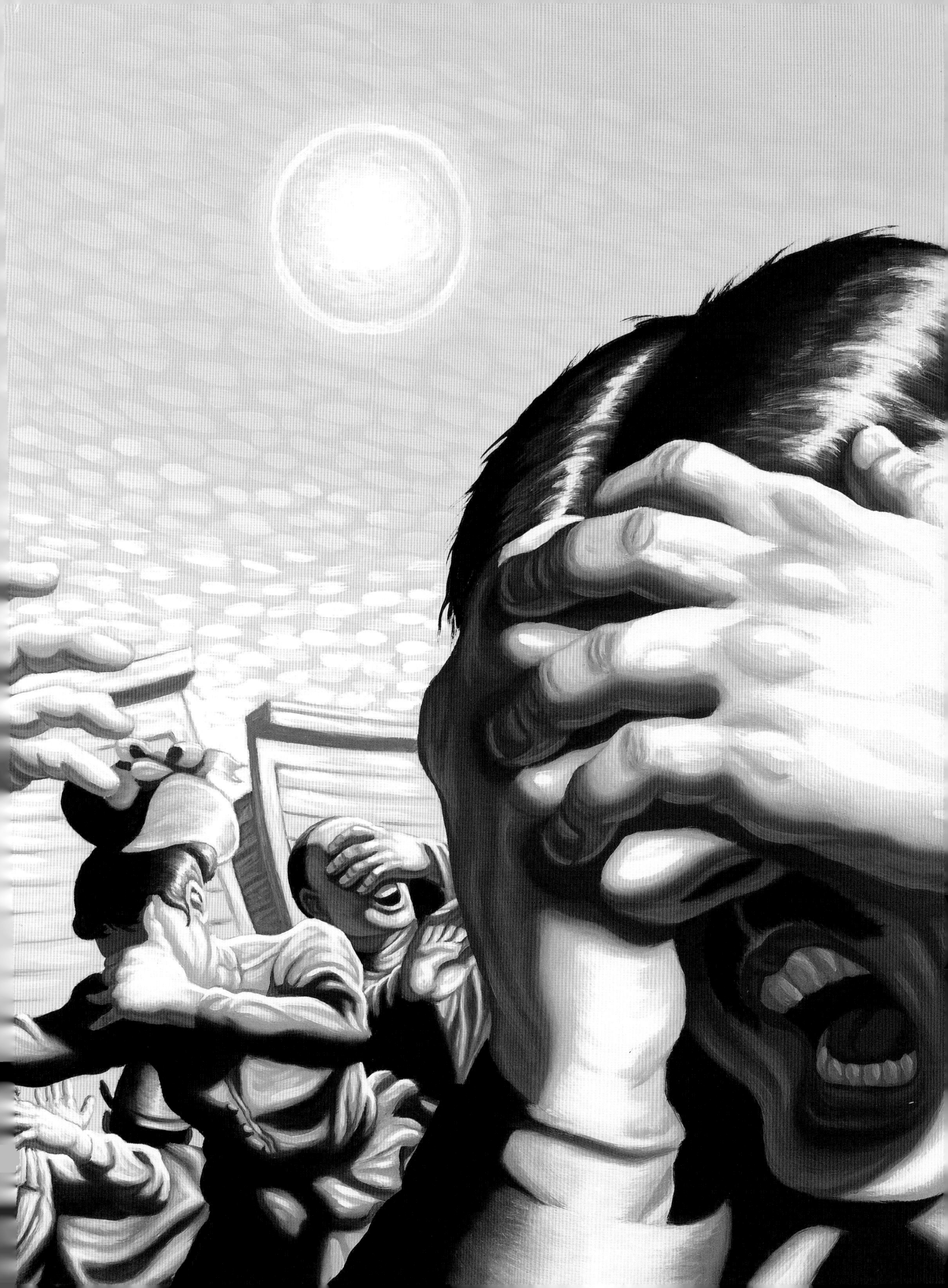

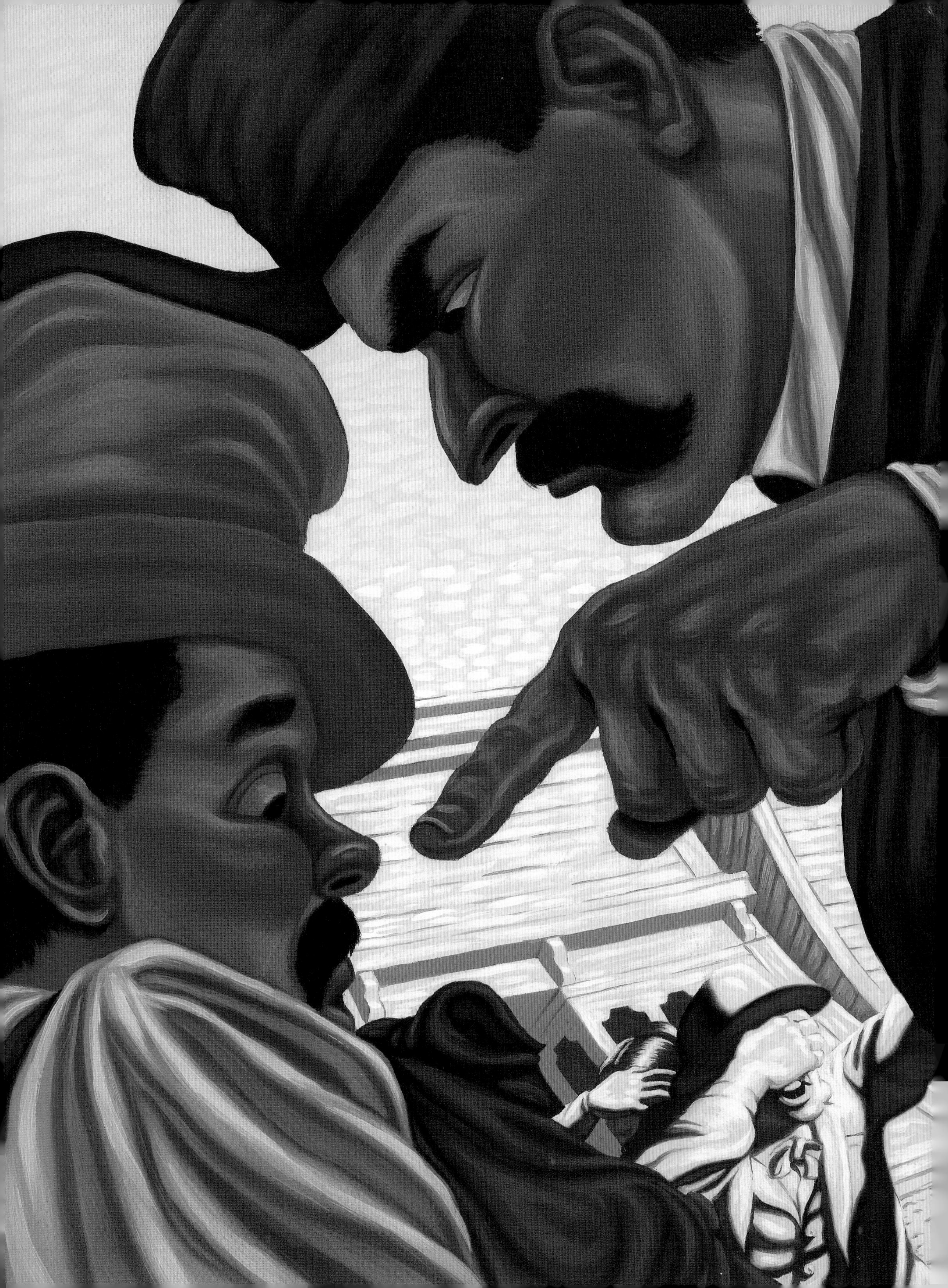

Sheriff Blackstone fired his gun into the air. "You can't hang Shoeshine Whittaker! Your shoes are shiny just like he guaranteed."

"But he made us all sick!" groaned someone in the crowd.

The sheriff turned to Shoeshine. "You've gone and made things too shiny. People's eyes are hurtin'. Reckon you'll have to pay the whole town's doctor bills, 'less you can think of somethin' else."

Shoeshine mumbled under his breath as he looked out over the town wonderin' what to do. Finally, he had an idea. "I can fix things, Sheriff. Have ever'one bring two bits and come down to the river."

Shoeshine hurried to the banks of the Mud River. Pretty soon, people started comin'.

"Line up here," shouted Shoeshine, "and wait your turn!" The people lined up at the sign, which read:

Dig
Your Own
Shine Duller
Only 25¢
a Bag

One by one, the townspeople gave Shoeshine their quarters. One by one, they took Shoeshine's shovel and dug up a small bit of mud, fillin' a square of cloth.

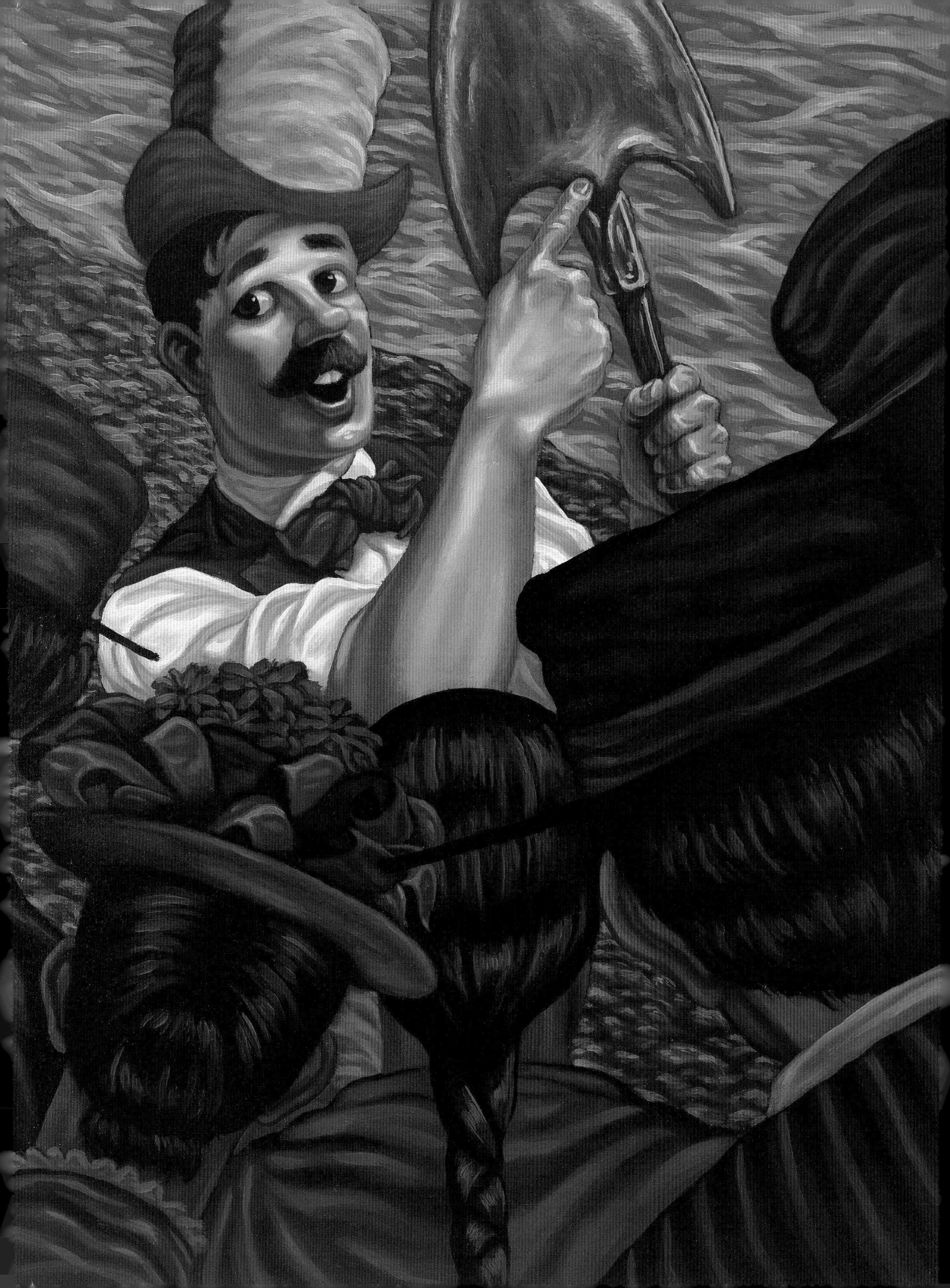

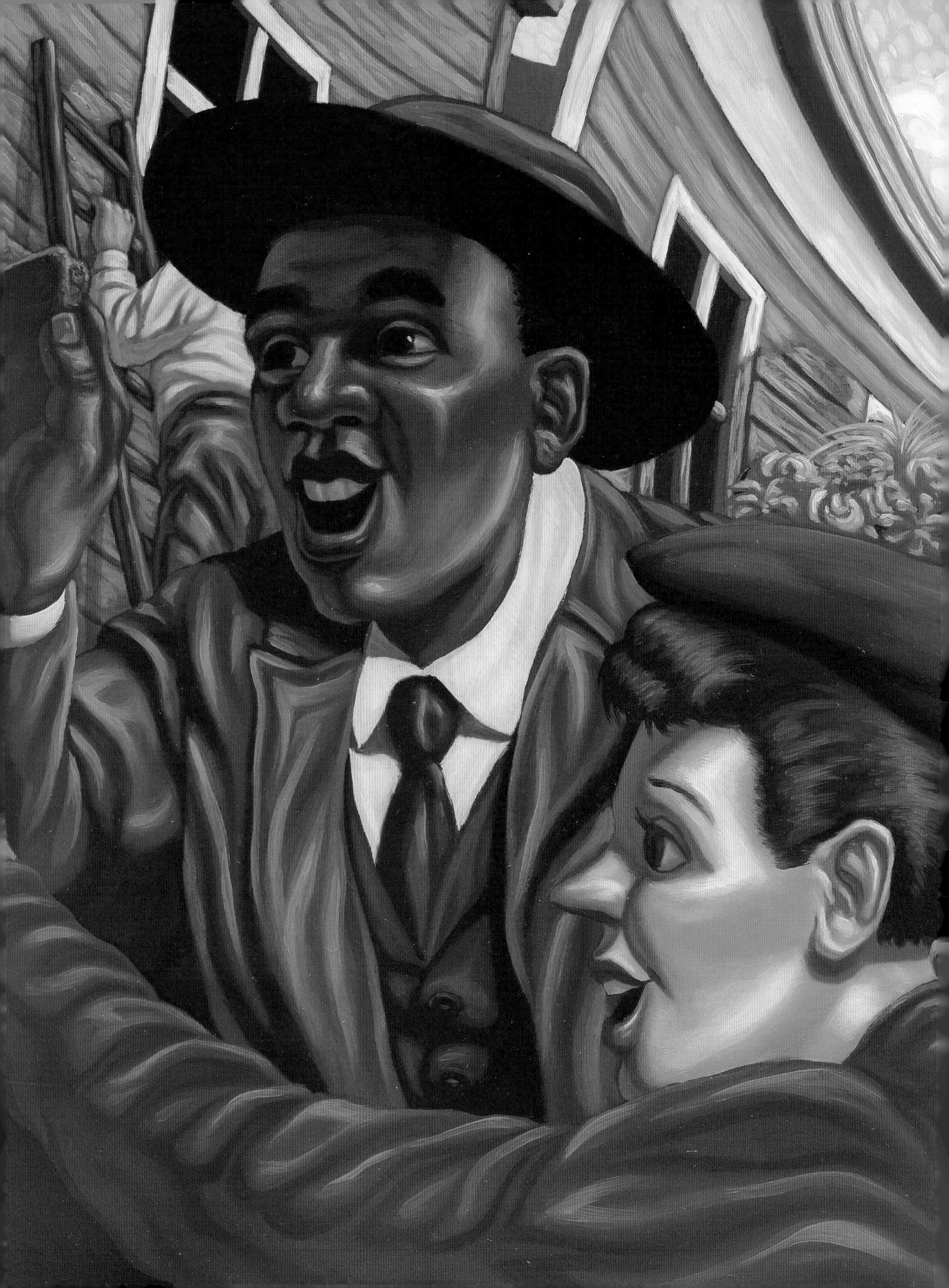

"You just take a rag and rub a bit of duller on any surface that's too shiny," announced Shoeshine. "Things'll be back to normal in no time, and that shine won't hurt your eyes anymore. Shoeshine Whittaker guarantees it!"

The people spent the rest of the day diggin' shine duller from the banks of the Mud River, and dullin' things up. By sunset, Mudville was back to normal.

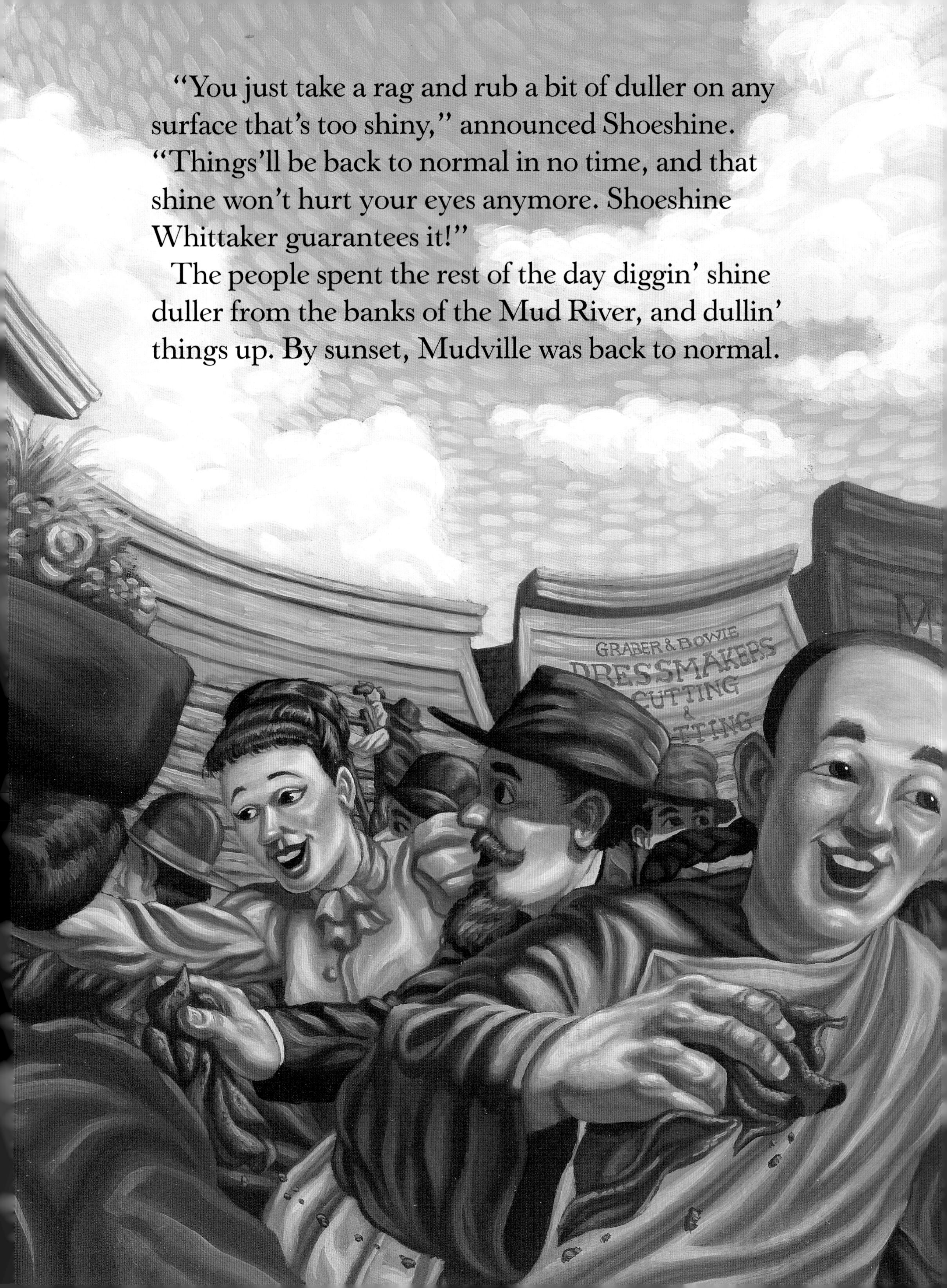
GRABER & BOWIE
DRESSMAKERS
CUTTING
&

Everyone waved to Shoeshine as he rode out of town. "You come back and visit us again, Shoeshine Whittaker," yelled Sheriff Blackstone.

Shoeshine listened to the clink of coins in his strong box as Miss Clara pulled the wagon down the road. "Shoeshine Whittaker guarantees it!" he called, wavin' his top hat.

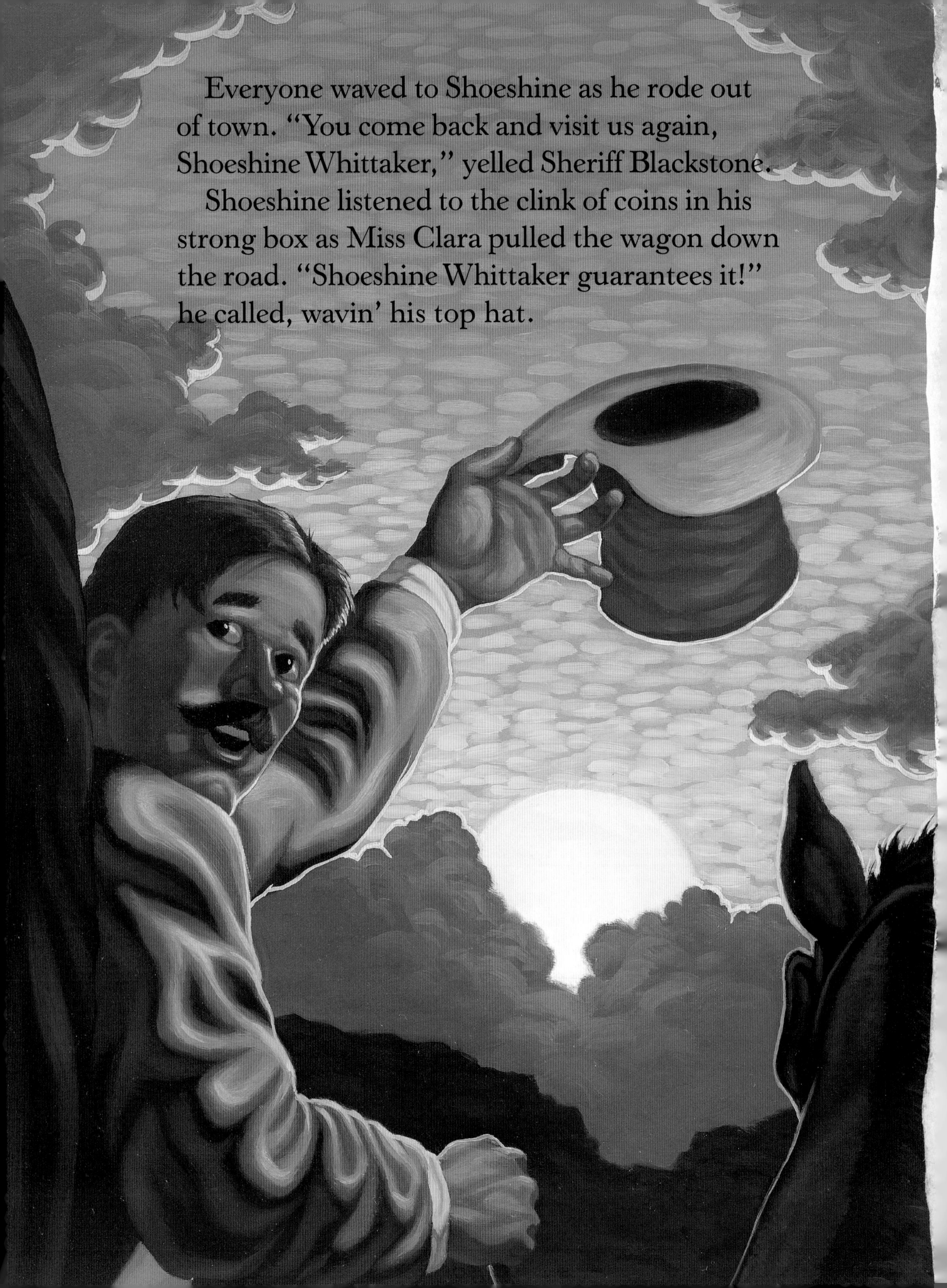